This book is a work of fiction. Any references to historical events, real people, or real places are used fictitiously. Other names, characters, places, and events are products of the author's imagination, and any resemblance to actual events or places or persons, living or dead, is entirely coincidental.

LITTLE SIMON
An imprint of Simon & Schuster Children's Publishing Division • 1230 Avenue of the Americas, New York, New York 10020 • First Little Simon paperback edition November 2016 • Copyright © 2016 by Simon & Schuster, Inc. All rights reserved, including the right of reproduction in whole or in part in any form. LITTLE SIMON is a registered trademark of Simon & Schuster, Inc., and associated colophon is a trademark of Simon & Schuster, Inc. For information about special discounts for bulk purchases, please contact Simon & Schuster Special Sales at 1-866-506-1949 or business@simonandschuster.com. The Simon & Schuster Speakers Bureau can bring authors to your live event. For more information or to book an event contact the Simon & Schuster Speakers Bureau at 1-866-248-3049 or visit our website at www.simonspeakers.com. Series designed by Laura Roode. Book designed by Hannah Frece. The text of this book was set in Usherwood.
Manufactured in the United States of America 0519 MTN
10 9 8 7 6 5 4
Cataloging-in-Publication Data is available for this title from the Library of Congress.
ISBN 978-1-4814-7149-7 (hc)
ISBN 978-1-4814-7148-0 (pbk)
ISBN 978-1-4814-7150-3 (eBook)

the adventures of
SOPHiE MOUSE

9

The Great Big Paw Print

By Poppy Green • Illustrated by Jennifer A. Bell

LITTLE SIMON

New York London Toronto Sydney New Delhi

CONTENTS

chapter 1

Stolen Apples

It was a Monday afternoon and school had just let out in Pine Needle Grove. Sophie Mouse and her little brother, Winston, ran together to their mother's bakery.

They knew that right around this time, Mrs. Mouse would have just baked something delicious. They also knew that she would let them try it!

And they were right. Mrs. Mouse
gave a warm apple fritter to both
Sophie and Winston.

"Thank you kids for coming to help out today," Mrs. Mouse told them. "There's always so much to do to get ready for winter!"

Every fall Mrs. Mouse stocked up on ingredients to bake with over the winter. Already she had canned her summer fruits: strawberries, blueberries, peaches, and plums.

But she still had lots of autumn fruits and vegetables to preserve: apples and pears, cranberries and beets, pumpkins and pomegranates. So she had asked Sophie and Winston for help. They could wash and peel and get everything ready.

"Can we come *every* day this week?" Winston asked, taking a bite of fritter.

Sophie smiled. She could guess *why* her brother wanted to come to the bakery every day!

"That would be a huge help," Mrs. Mouse said, winking at Sophie.

So every day that week, Sophie and Winston hurried to the bakery just as soon as school let out.

Before they got to work, they'd sit on stools at the

counter. Mrs. Mouse would serve them a treat fresh from the oven. And Sophie and Winston would tell her about their day.

On Tuesday, Mrs. Mouse made cranberry tarts. Sophie nibbled as she explained that her day was *okay*.

"It was supposed to be library day," Sophie said. "But Mrs. Wise said

the library is closed. It needs some kind of 'emergency fix-up.'"

"Hmm," said Mrs. Mouse. "I hadn't heard. I wonder what happened."

On Wednesday, Mrs. Mouse served up pumpkin spice scones.

Meanwhile, Winston gabbed about the secret code he and his friend James were making up and a strange rustling he'd heard in the woods near the school. Sophie told Winston he was probably just imagining it.

On Thursday, Mrs. Mouse gave Sophie and Winston cinnamon doughnuts.

"Tomorrow is Apple Math Day!" Winston announced to his mother.

"We each bring in a couple of apples," explained Sophie. "We'll sort them by color. We'll graph how many there are of each color. And *then* we'll taste them all!"

On Friday, Sophie and Winston arrived later than usual.

They plopped down into the stools.
Their shoulders drooped.

Sophie looked down at the plate
Mrs. Mouse had put out for them. On
it were two pastries.

"They're called bear claws," said Mrs. Mouse. "It's a brand-new recipe."

The pastries *did* have the same shape as bear paw prints.

But Sophie didn't feel like eating.

Not until they
shared their news.

"Our apples
disappeared!"
Winston blurted out.

Sophie nodded. "We left them out
on the picnic table while we had our
morning lesson inside. But when we
came out for
Apple Math,
they were
gone."

"You can't do Apple Math without apples!" Winston cried.

Mrs. Mouse gave them each a hug. "How disappointing," she said gently.

"I know how excited you were about Apple Math Day."

Sophie *was* very disappointed. But she was also very confused. "We looked all over for them," Sophie said. "But they were just *gone*. It's almost like someone . . . *took* them."

chapter 2

A Visit with Pippa

In the Mouse family's house in the hollow of the big oak tree, Sophie was almost done with her Saturday morning chores.

She had made her bed. She had swept the upstairs hallway.

She had even helped her dad tidy up the root cellar. The shelves were packed with jars of jams, jellies, and

sauces. The bins were full of carrots and potatoes. They would last a long while in the cellar.

"I'd say we're almost set for the winter," George Mouse said. He stacked the pickles two jars high. Now there was space for a few more.

Sophie finished putting the spice containers in alphabetical order.

When she was done, Sophie asked her dad if she could go play. She and Hattie and Owen wanted to visit their friend Pippa the hedgehog. "Any day now, she'll be going to sleep for the winter," Sophie explained.

Mr. Mouse agreed, and Sophie ran off to pick up her friends. Soon, the three of them were on their way to Hickory Hill, where Pippa lived with her family.

"I hope we can find her house," Hattie said.

They hadn't seen Pippa since the previous winter when they'd met her. Sophie had accidentally crashed into Pippa's house with her sled! The noise had woken Pippa from her winter sleep.

"Hickory Hill looks so different without snow," Owen remarked when they got there. The grassy hill was covered with

late-season wildflowers.

They peeked into the underbrush at the edge of the woods. "Hello?" Sophie called out. "Pippa? It's us! Sophie—"

"And Owen!" cried Owen.

"And Hattie!" Hattie added.

They stood silently, listening for
a reply.

Then they heard a rustling. A
small voice called back, "Hello? Hello!
Where are you?"

Sophie called out again. "Follow
the sound of my voice!" she said.

Moments later, a little head covered in spiky brown fur poked out of the underbrush.

"Pippa!" Sophie, Hattie, and Owen shouted.

"Haaa!" Pippa exclaimed. "Ooo! Mmm shh fro whood fru shee ooo!"

Sophie looked at Owen and Hattie. "What did she say?"

Hattie and Owen shrugged.

Pippa ran up to

them. "Ho hm frooo beh?" she said excitedly.

Sophie forced a smile. She couldn't understand Pippa. Was this some sort of hedgehog language they didn't know?

How could they all play together if they couldn't understand one another?

What was going on?

— chapter 3 —

A Great Big Paw Print

For a moment, they stood in awkward silence.

Then Sophie noticed Pippa was chewing. Her mouth was stuffed with berries.

No wonder! thought Sophie. *She was trying to talk with her mouth full!*

Pippa gulped them down and

then giggled. "Let me try saying that again. I said, 'It's so good to see you! How have you been?'"

Before Sophie could answer, Pippa added, "Oh! How rude of me. Would you like some berries?" She opened her paw to reveal a few more.

The friends laughed.

"Don't be silly," said Hattie. "You

need it! You're filling up for your winter sleep!"

Sophie nodded. "We're filling up at our house, too," she said. "Except

we're filling up our *pantry*. You have to fill up your *tummy*!"

Pippa ate her last few berries. Then she motioned for the others to follow her. "Come on! You have to meet my family!" Pippa said.

The friends followed Pippa through the underbrush. Before long, they came to a mound of dry leaves and grass. Sophie remembered this: it was Pippa's house!

Six more hedgehogs sat eating together out front. At first, they seemed alarmed to see strangers. But Pippa said: "Everyone! These are the snow-day friends I told you about!"

Pippa introduced her mother and father, and her sisters and brothers:

Penny, Peter, Pearl, and Percy.

Pearl, the youngest, tugged at Sophie's leggings. "Can you *really* make a mouse out of snow?" she asked.

Sophie, Hattie, and Owen laughed.

Clearly Pippa had told Pearl all about their snow adventures.

Sophie smiled. "I sure can!" she replied.

Pippa's parents invited the guests to join them for a snack.

"Actually," said Sophie, "we were

hoping Pippa could come play for a little bit."

"Oh, can I?" Pippa asked her parents excitedly.

"Of course," Pippa's mom said.

So the friends headed for Forget-Me-Not Lake.

"Remember last time?" Sophie said as they walked.

"The lake was frozen," Hattie said.

"We went ice skating!" Owen added. "Or tried to. Right, Pippa? Uh, Pippa?"

They stopped and looked back.

Pippa was way behind. She was nib-
bling on some seeds she'd found.

Sophie, Hattie, and Owen waited
patiently as Pippa chewed.

"Sorry!" Pippa said, hurrying to
catch up.

They walked a dozen more steps—
until Pippa spotted some mushrooms.

She stopped for another mouthful.

The others stopped too.

It happened again and again. They walked a bit. Pippa stopped for a snack. They walked a bit more.

All in all, there was more eating than walking.

Hattie turned to whisper in Sophie's ear as they walked. "This might take a while. I wonder—aah!"

Hattie wasn't looking where she

was going and she fell right into a shallow ditch in the path!

"Hattie!" Sophie cried. "Are you okay?" She climbed down to help her friend.

Hattie stood up, brushing dirt off her skirt. "Oh, I'm fine," she said.

"But who dug this ditch *right* in the middle of the path?"

Up on higher ground, Owen was looking at the full size of this "ditch."

"Actually," Owen said, "I don't think that's a ditch. . . ."

"What do you mean?" Sophie asked.

"I think it's a paw print," Owen said. "Come look."

Sophie and Hattie scrambled up to stand next to Owen.

Now Sophie could see the whole thing. "You're right," she told Owen.

"That *is* a paw print. A great big paw print!"

Sophie studied it. The shape looked so *familiar*.

Sophie's stomach suddenly grumbled. She gasped. That was it! The paw print looked like the pastry at her mom's bakery.

All of a sudden, Sophie knew!

"A bear claw!" she cried.

chapter 4

Following in Someone's Footsteps

"A bear claw?!" the other three animals asked at the same time.

Bears lived in Silverlake Forest. Everyone knew that.

But not everyone in Silverlake Forest had *met* one.

Sophie nodded. "Definitely. I've

never seen a bear paw print before but this looks exactly like the bear claw pastries my mom has been making."

"What—what should we do?" asked Hattie nervously.

Suddenly, Pippa spoke up. "I just remembered! My dad said he's met a bear family around here," she told them. "I'm pretty sure he said they seemed friendly. And they hibernate for winter just like us, so maybe this bear is already sleeping!"

That seemed to relieve Hattie a bit.

"Well, let's go to Forget-Me-Not Lake," Sophie suggested. "And we can all keep an eye out . . . just in case," she added.

So the friends continued on.

Finally, they arrived at the water's edge. Pippa found a comfy spot to graze in a bed of lemon clover. Sophie picked up stones and tried to skip them on the water. Hattie hopscotched across lily pads.

Owen dipped his tail into the lake
and shivered. "Brrrr . . . ," he said.
"It's already too cold to swim!"

The friends were silent for a little
while.

Sophie was lost in thought,

imagining what it might be like to run into a bear. Surely, there might be nice bears. After all, everyone was afraid of Owen when he arrived at Pine Needle Grove because he was a snake and they'd heard scary stories about snakes. But Owen was one of the nicest animals Sophie had ever met. But what if the bear came to Pine Needle Grove? What would they do?

"Sophie? Sophie?"

All three animals were looking at Sophie.

"Oh—sorry!" Sophie said.

"Daydreaming again?" Hattie asked with a knowing smile. Sophie nodded sheepishly.

"We were asking if you want to play a game," Pippa told her.

So the friends played for a while. They looked for glittery rocks at the lake edge. They drew in the mud with sticks.

Pippa would begin each activity with them. But after a

few minutes, she would take a snack break.

In the end, the friends just chatted, with Pippa snacking, and Sophie, Hattie, and Owen lazing on rocks nearby.

When Pippa started to yawn, the animals decided it was time to go home.

"I've been getting tired earlier and earlier every day," Pippa said, as she got up and stretched. "So I know it must almost be hibernation time!"

As the friends said good-bye, Sophie promised they'd come visit Pippa in the spring.

"Bye, everyone!" Pippa called as she walked toward her home.

Sophie, Hattie, and Owen waved good-bye until they couldn't see Pippa anymore.

It was still early in the afternoon. The friends decided to take a different route home—the long way

around the lake.

They kept the water in sight the whole way. They tromped through a bunch of white birch trees. They balanced on log bridges across streams.

Then they walked up a little hill. Sophie suddenly stopped at the top. Hattie and Owen did, too.

Down below, on the other side of the hill, was another bear track. It was partially hidden by leaves. But Sophie recognized it immediately.

"Should—should we

keep going?" Hattie asked.

Sophie was less confident this time, but she knew she had to be brave for Hattie. "I guess we were bound to see another one," she said. "Right?"

Owen nodded. The three friends walked on.

A dozen paces later, they saw another bear track.

And then another.

And then *another*.

"Okaaaay,"
said Hattie. "So
a bear definitely
came this way."

"But we don't know
when," Sophie
pointed out.
"It could have
been a long time ago."
The friends walked
and they walked. And every
so often, they saw another paw print.
It was almost as if *they* were follow-
ing *the bear*!
Then they came around a bend.

In the distance Sophie could make out Oak Hollow Theater through the trees. That meant they were getting close to town.

And so were the bear tracks.

"Do you think . . . ?" Hattie began.

Sophie knew what her friend was thinking. "There's a bear in town?"

chapter 5

Mystery at the Library

Somewhere between the theater and the library, Sophie, Hattie, and Owen lost the paw prints. The bear tracks had been getting fainter each time, and soon the friends could not find any more.

Sophie shrugged. "Oh well."

"Maybe the bear turned off in another direction?" Hattie suggested.

"You know what?" Owen said. "If there *were* a bear in town, I'm sure we'd know. I mean, I think it would be obvious."

Sophie laughed. "Yeah," she said. "I think the bear would probably be hard to miss!"

"So that solves it!" cried Hattie happily. "No bear in town!"

They weren't far from the library. Sophie wanted to check to see if it

had reopened yet. But Owen had to get home. So the friends said goodbye and parted ways.

An OPEN sign was hanging on the door of the library! "Yay!" Sophie cheered as she pushed on the door.

Inside, the library looked just as it usually did. The books lined the floor-to-ceiling

shelves. The chairs at the reading tables were neatly pushed in. The wooden floors gleamed.

Sophie and Hattie browsed the young reader section. They didn't seem to have the newest Mystery Mouse book. But Sophie found a novel about a pirate squirrel that sounded good. Hattie chose a fantasy story set in a floating city.

"Oooh," said Sophie, peeking at Hattie's book. "Not at all a practical choice. Good for you, Hattie!"

Hattie laughed. "You're rubbing off on me, Sophie Mouse."

They took their books to the counter. The librarian, Ms. Reeve, checked them out. She stamped the due date onto a card on the inside back cover.

Then she handed the books to Sophie and Hattie.

Sophie turned to go, but then she suddenly

wheeled back around. "Oh, Ms. Reeve! What was the 'emergency cleanup' for?"

Ms. Reeve leaned over the counter. "It was the strangest thing," she said. "I was the first one here that morning. I noticed that the back door was already open. And when I walked in, the place was a mess! The trash cans were knocked over, some of the trash had blown into other parts of the library, and some of the bookshelves had even been knocked over."

Sophie and Hattie exchanged puzzled looks.

"That's odd," Hattie said. "What do you think happened?"

Ms. Reeve shrugged. "I still don't know. But the *only* thing missing was some leftover cake from the party we'd had for another librarian's birthday that day!"

"That *is* strange," Sophie said. "Well, I'm glad everything's back to normal!" she told Ms. Reeve.

She and Hattie said good-bye and then turned to go.

But something was on Sophie's

mind. The missing apples. The fact that the *only* thing taken from the library was the leftover cake. The paw prints. Was there a connection?

Sophie thought she knew the answer.

chapter 6

Thief with a Sweet Tooth

Sophie's mind was racing a mile a minute.

"Hattie," she said. "I have an idea."

Hattie's brow furrowed. Sophie had quite the imagination, so Hattie could never be sure what her next idea would be.

"It seems like someone in town is hungry," Sophie continued. "Hungry

enough to look for food in a library. And hungry enough to take Apple Math apples."

"Maybe someone who is getting ready to hibernate?" Hattie said, catching Sophie's drift.

"Exactly," said Sophie.

The whole way home, Sophie and

Hattie talked it over. They couldn't be sure, but all the pieces seemed to fit: the library mess, the stolen apples.

And Sophie remembered the rustling Winston had heard in the woods. "I told him he was imagining it," said Sophie. "But maybe he wasn't."

They had reached Sophie's house.

"But if bears are *nice*," said Hattie, "wouldn't this one just ask for food? Why would he be stealing?"

Sophie shook her head. "I don't know."

Just then they heard footsteps coming through the woods. Mrs. Mouse was walking quickly up the path. Sophie thought she looked upset.

"Oh, Sophie," Mrs. Mouse called out. "Do me a favor? Please get your dad and Winston. And could you all come to the bakery?" She sighed a heavy sigh. "I'm going to need help— lots of help."

"Mom?" Sophie said. "What happened?"

"I don't really know," Mrs. Mouse replied. "I left to get milk at the general store. And when I got back—" Mrs. Mouse threw up her hands.

"Let's just say the bakery is a mess.
And *all* of my baked goods are
gone!"

Sophie and Hattie stared at each
other. Could it be . . . ?

Before they could say a word,

Mrs. Mouse turned and went back the way she'd come.

"I'll find my dad," Sophie said.

"I'm coming too!" said Hattie.

As soon as they heard the news, Mr. Mouse and Winston headed off to the bakery.

Hattie thought she should let her parents know where she was going, so Sophie went with

Hattie to her house.

But Mr. and Mrs. Frog weren't home. Hattie left a note.

Then the two of them hurried off.

"Shouldn't we tell your mom and dad about the bear tracks?" Hattie said as they walked.

Going to the bakery with Sophie. Be home soon. -Hattie

Sophie nodded. "I'll tell them as soon as we get there."

They were halfway to town. Something at the edge of the path caught Sophie's eye. She almost missed it, they were walking so fast. But she stopped to get a closer look.

It was a bear print!

No, wait! Sophie started laughing. It was way too tiny to be a bear

paw print. It was a bear *claw*—one
of her mom's pastries.

"Well, well, well," said Sophie.
"Maybe we have a *new* trail to
follow."

— chapter 7 —

The Nose Knows

Sophie and Hattie searched the area. They were looking for more pastries.

Sophie took a few steps off the path and into the trees.

Sure enough, ten paces in, Sophie found something else. She sniffed it. "Cinnamon doughnut," Sophie said.

"Wow, Sophie!" Hattie exclaimed. "How did you find that?"

Sophie thought about it for a moment. "I smelled it!" she realized. "My nose led me to it."

After all, mice *did* have an amazing sense of smell.

Sophie sniffed around some more, letting her nose lead her. Hattie followed. They ducked under branches

and pushed through underbrush.

Suddenly she stopped, bent down, and moved some dry leaves aside. Underneath was a tart!

"Cranberry," said Sophie. "I'm sure of it."

Further on, she sniffed out a pump-kin spice scone.

They came out of the trees onto a footpath.

"This is the way to the schoolhouse,"
Hattie said, pointing down the path.

But Sophie dove back into the
woods on the other side.

She found an apple fritter.

Further on, she found a
puzzling one: "Either a
Boston creme dough-
nut or an eclair,"
she decided. "Hard
to tell which."

Then Sophie
found lots of
crumbs all around
the base of a tree. But

that's where the trail went cold. She
walked in a circle, hoping to catch
another scent.

Sophie stopped and leaned on the
tree trunk. "I guess we've hit a dead
end," she said to Hattie.

Just then something fell out of the

tree onto Sophie's head. "Oof!" she cried, startled. She reached up to see what had landed on her.

Holding it out for Hattie to see, Sophie whispered, "Blueberry muffin!"

They heard a rustle in the tree above them. They looked up. As they did, something else fell down. It bounced off Sophie's nose and fell to the ground.

Sophie picked it up. "A piece of a gingersnap!" she whispered.

The rustling up above continued.

"It's in the tree!" Hattie whispered.

Sophie nodded. "It sure is," she whispered back. "And I'm going up there." Without another word, she scurried up the bark to the first branch.

"Sophie, wait!" Hattie whispered.

But Sophie's curiosity was stronger than her fear. She kept climbing. She cleared the second and third branches. The rustling was getting louder. She was getting closer!

The higher Sophie got, the more autumn leaves there were still on the branches. She passed the fourth and fifth branches. But she still couldn't see the source of the rustling.

As Sophie cleared the sixth branch, she couldn't see through all the leaves to the other side. Sophie

paused for a moment, listening. It was silent.

Slowly, Sophie poked her head through the leaves.

She froze.

A large, wet, black nose was inches away from her own. She was face-to-face with a bear.

Sophie opened her mouth to call down to Hattie.

"HEEEEEEEEEELLLP!"

But the voice she heard wasn't her own.

It was the bear's.

— chapter 8 —

Wooly Bear

The tree branch was shaking. The bear was quivering with fright!

"Oh, please," he whimpered to Sophie. "Oh, please, don't hurt me."

He was trying to inch away from Sophie. But he was already squished up against the tree trunk.

Sophie could see now that he was just a bear cub. He was still enormous compared to Sophie. But he looked young—and so scared! Sophie's heart warmed to him right away.

"Don't worry," Sophie said gently. "I'm not going to hurt you."

The bear was still shaking. He eyed Sophie warily.

"I promise," Sophie said. "My name is Sophie. What's yours?"

The bear didn't answer right away. Sophie noticed that he was holding a

doughnut. She was struck by how small it looked in his large paws. He popped the whole thing in his mouth like it was nothing. "My name is Wooly," he answered after he had finished chewing. "Wooly Bear."

"Hi, Wooly!" Sophie replied. "Aren't those doughnuts good? My mom makes the best ones. She owns the bakery in town."

Wooly stared at Sophie. His bottom lip started to tremble. Then all of a sudden, he began to cry. The noise startled Sophie, who almost fell out of the tree.

"Oh, I'm *so* sorry," Wooly wailed. "I took them without asking. I was just so hungry. And scared. I don't know how to get home, and it's almost time to hibernate. And I didn't know what to do!" Wooly stopped crying long enough to eat another doughnut he had stashed away. "And did I

mention: I'm just soooo hungry!"

Sophie nodded. "I know. I have a hedgehog friend named Pippa. She hibernates, too. And she's *really*

hungry right now, just like you." She smiled at Wooly. "So I understand."

"You do?" Wooly said.

"Yep," said Sophie. "And you know what else? I think my friends and I can help you get home."

Wooly jumped up. This time, *he* almost fell out of the tree. "Really?" he exclaimed. "But how? How do you know where I live?"

Sophie motioned for Wooly to climb down with her. "Come on," she said. "Come meet my friends. We'll tell you all about it."

wooly comes clean

Wooly wiped his eyes. "Oh—okay," he said. "Do you want a ride down?" he asked Sophie.

"Sure!" she exclaimed. She climbed on top of his head and clung to his fur.

When they were down on the ground, Hattie was there, nervously waiting.

Hattie jumped back. "Uh . . . , Sophie?" she said.

"It's okay, Hattie! This is Wooly," Sophie reassured her friend.

Wooly greeted Hattie with a shy wave.

Then Sophie explained to Wooly about the first paw print they'd seen—way over near Hickory Hill.

"Then we saw more tracks," she continued. "They went from Forget-Me-Not Lake to the edge of town."

Hattie chimed in. "I bet your house is somewhere between the lake and Hickory Hill," she suggested.

"I *do* live near a lake!" Wooly exclaimed. "Could you take me there? I bet I'll be able to find my home!"

"Sure!" Sophie said. "We can go right now!"

Sophie and Hattie started walking. But Wooly hesitated.

"Before I go," he said, looking at Sophie, "um . . ." He trailed off.

"What is it, Wooly?" Sophie asked.

"I was wondering if I could say sorry to your mom. And . . . some other animals too."

Sophie nodded. "It's okay. We know. About the library? And the apples?"

Wooly nodded bashfully.

Hattie smiled. "Some of the apples

were ours," she said. "We already forgive you."

Sophie led Wooly toward the bakery. Meanwhile, Hattie ran off to get Owen. She knew he would want to meet Wooly too!

In town, lots of the animals stared or did a double take when they saw Wooly.

Sophie could tell it was making Wooly uncomfortable. But she assured him that it was okay. People just

weren't used to seeing bears around here!

When they got to the bakery, Sophie told Wooly to wait outside.

"Mom? Dad? Winston?" Sophie called. "I have someone for you to meet!" Sophie led her family outside.

Winston let out a high-pitched squeal and ran behind his parents.

"Winston,

it's okay!" Sophie said. "Guys, this is
Wooly." Sophie then explained what
had happened and why Wooly was
so hungry.

"I'm so sorry, Mrs. Mouse," Wooly said sincerely. "I shouldn't have taken your pastries without asking."

"It's okay, Wooly," Mrs. Mouse said. "None of the animals in Pine Needle Grove need to hibernate in winter, so we're not quite used to it. But I *did* just bake some rosemary sugar cookies. Would you like to be my taste-tester?"

Wooly beamed. "I'd love to!"

At the library, Ms. Reeve was also understanding. "Actually, it's a relief to have the mystery solved!" she said. "You're forgiven, Wooly."

Then, with a deep sigh of relief, Wooly turned to Sophie. "Okay. I'm ready to go home now. Will you take me?"

Just then, Hattie and Owen came running up. "Can we come, too?" Hattie called.

Sophie and Hattie introduced Wooly to Owen, and Wooly thanked

them all for helping him get home.

The three friends led the way out of town. Wooly followed. But with just a few steps, he was already ahead of them.

Wooly's strides were so large! For every one of his, Sophie had to take about a dozen.

Wooly stopped and waited for the smaller animals to catch up. "You know what?" he

said to the other animals. "I think I know a faster way to get there. Climb on!" He bent down so the friends could climb onto his back.

They hadn't gone too far when Wooly recognized where they were. "I know how to get home from here!" he exclaimed happily. He thanked Sophie, Hattie, and Owen for helping him as they climbed back down.

"Come and visit us!" Sophie called as the trio turned to go home. Now she had another friend to look forward to seeing in the springtime!

The End

Here's a peek at the next
Adventures of Sophie Mouse book!

Sophie Mouse ran to the window. She looked up at the sky. The clouds looked darker than the last time she'd checked. Sophie stretched her hand outside. No rain drops.

"It's not raining yet!" Sophie cried, running back into the kitchen. Her whiskers were tingling. She could tell the rain was coming. But maybe there was just enough time for their picnic.

In the Mouse family's house at the base of the oak tree, Mrs. Mouse had made her famous vanilla-bean scones. The sweet scent of the vanilla filled the kitchen.

"Okay! Let's go!" Sophie exclaimed.

She picked up the picnic basket. Winston grabbed the blanket. And the Mouse family stepped outside.

Plip! Plop! Plip!

Sophie felt three big raindrops— one on her ear, one on her shoulder, and one on the tip of her nose.

the adventures of
SOPHIE MOUSE

For excerpts, activities, and more about
these adorable tales & tails, visit
AdventuresofSophieMouse.com!